KT-153-739

A VERY BRAVE Witch

Alison McGHEE   Harry BLISS

Simon and Schuster
New York London Toronto Sydney New Delhi

SIMON AND SCHUSTER

First published in Great Britain in 2014 by Simon and Schuster UK Ltd

1st Floor, 222 Gray's Inn Road, London, WC1X 8HB

A CBS Company

Published in the USA in 2006 by Simon & Schuster Books for Young Readers,

an imprint of Simon and Schuster Children's Publishing Division, New York

Text copyright © 2006, 2014 by Alison McGhee

Cover & Illustrations copyright © 2006, 2014 by Harry Bliss

The rights of Alison McGhee and Harry Bliss to be identified as the author and illustrator of this

work has been asserted by them in accordance with the Copyright, Designs and Patents Act, 1988

All rights reserved, including the right of reproduction in whole or in part in any form

A CIP catalogue record for this book is available from the British Library upon request

ISBN: 978-1-4711-2305-4 (PB)

ISBN: 978-1-4711-2306-1 (ebook)

Printed in China

1 3 5 7 9 10 8 6 4 2

www.simonandschuster.co.uk

To Holly McGhee – A. M.

For Charley and Ben Bliss – H. B.

KEEP
OUT

It's time for
this brave witch
to take a closer look.
Hang on, Kitty,
we're going in!
WINSLOW
HOMER
RIP

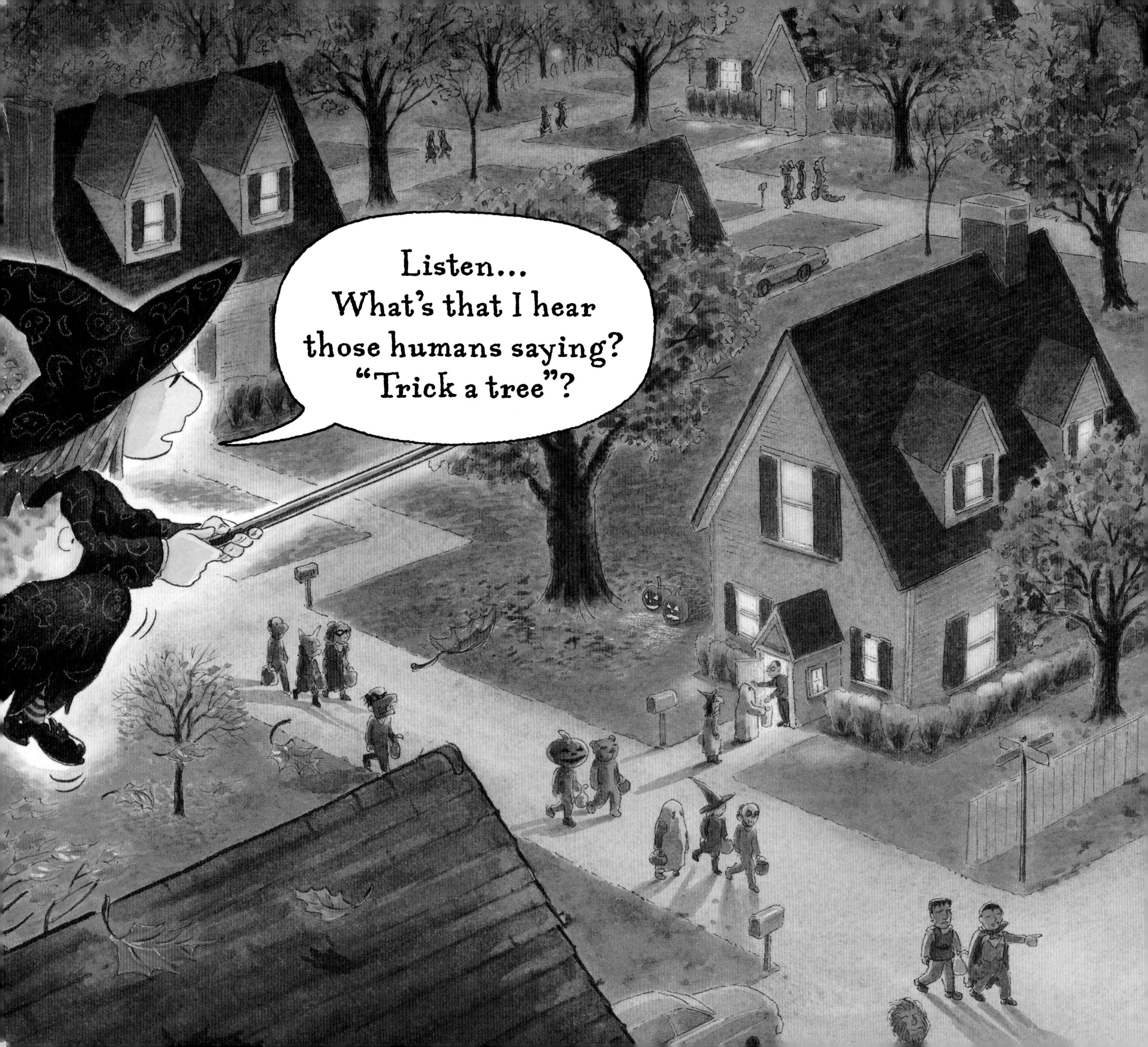
Listen...
What's that I hear
those humans saying?
"Trick a tree"?

Some witches, the very brave ones, are not afraid of humans.
And some humans, the very brave ones, are not afraid to fly.